'Til Death Do Us Part

by

KAREN J. OSTBY

Trafford
PUBLISHING™

DEDICATION

In memory of Joyce, whose life was tragically cut short at a young age, and who inspired this story.

ACKNOWLEDGMENTS

No task is ever completed without the support, encouragement, and assistance from others. Writing Til Death Do Us Part was a mission supported by the efforts of many therefore,

My very special thanks to "Veronica Schnelle" and "Walt Nomack" (you know who you are) for making available important background information and for giving of their time so generously.

Thanks to "Veronica Schnelle" for supplying the impetus for this story.

Special thanks to my consultants at Trafford Publishing, Greg Galbraith and Jennifer Bradley.

My very special thanks to my "editors": Judith Cummings Camp, Vicki Cummings, Lissa Eade, Gail G, Madelyn Jones, Shirley Keezing and Barbara Kiesel for your ideas, editing, support and encouragement.

Thank you my friends who supplied ideas, names of possible contacts and encouragement: Helen Boule, Helen K and Lynne Sandahl.

Thank you, Jeffrey Kinbghorn for your initial advice.

Thank you, John Keppler for your support and continual encouragement throughout this experience.

Thank you, CT. State Police Investigative Officer, Daniel Cargil and Retired CT. State Police Officer, Robert Rasmussen for your assistance.

CONTENTS

PROLOGUE
7

PART 1
THE PAST
9

PART 2
THE PRESENT
41

EPILOGUE
61

PROLOGUE

"Her golden hair symbolizes her sunny personality." Joan's yearbook quote described her to a tee. How then did she end up accused of suicide, unable to defend herself? Would someone with a sunny personality do such a thing? Would she leave two babies and the family with whom she grew up? Surely Joan never thought her life would end this way, for she was only twenty, four months shy of her twenty-first birthday. It's likely she dreamed of living a long life and days filled with work, marriage, children, grandchildren and retirement with her husband. Those dreams changed as Joan fulfilled only a few of them during her short life that was snuffed out so abruptly in the spring of 1963.

How could her life change so fast? She had everything a girl could want. She married her handsome, dark-haired, high school sweetheart and gave birth to two beautiful baby boys. She loved their cute little house and her secretarial job for the few months she worked. She had everything she wanted, hadn't she? What happened to alter her life and ultimately, to destroy Joan's dreams?

7

PART 1

THE PAST

Spring had finally arrived in Martinsburg. The birds returned, the early crocus, daffodils and some tulips blossomed. The flowers Joan planted in the fall bloomed in the front of her house. It was April 19, 1963. It was going to be a cool but beautiful day to take her babies out for a walk in their double stroller and then go to the grocery store with her sister-in-law, Barbara. She bathed the boys and dressed Kenny in his size one-year shirt and overalls and Danny in his size six-month-old shirt and pants that they were rapidly outgrowing. She put them in their cribs while she got herself ready. She was clothed except for putting on a dress. It was the kind of day that made one feel hopeful about the future. Something had to change for the better. Spring coming was like a fresh start.

Joan heard a door open; it must be my husband Albert she thought. What was he doing back here at 1 P.M. Did he forget to take something with him? "Albert is that you? I'm surprised you're home. Did you forget something?" she asked.

A figure pointed a pistol at her. Who was it? Was it a man or a woman? She couldn't tell from the clothes. She couldn't see the face. It was covered by a stocking mask. She saw dark hair and noticed he or she was wearing gloves. "What are you doing? Put down the gun! What do you want?" She shouted. "Do you want money? I'll give it to you. Don't shoot. Don't hurt my babies. You can have whatever you want." She shouted. "Do you want my car? Wait, I'll get the keys." The figure shook his or her head. "Please don't shoot." Joan screamed as the figure moved forward, NO! Please don't kill me!"

Joan tried to push the figure away when it got closer to her but it hit her hard a couple of times and she fell to the floor. She was stunned. She couldn't get up fast enough. She tried to get out of the way. She crawled toward the bathroom and slumped to the floor. It was too late. The figure fired one bullet that missed her and hit the wall. She tried to move back. Another bullet flew by and it missed her too. She had to keep moving to dodge any more bullets, but how? She lay there, just inside the bathroom door, frozen by fear. A third round was fired; it hit Joan in the bull's eye of her forehead. Blood gushed and poured from her head, over her face. Her long hair fell over her face and sopped up blood like a mop. The figure moved her and felt for her pulse twice, on her neck and wrist. Joan barely felt herself losing consciousness and then, she was gone.

Kenny and Danny had been crying but by now they were wailing. They must've heard their mother's screams and pleas.

D. Albert took a call from one of his children. The worker who called him to the phone wasn't sure who was calling. The voice on the other end was shouting and sounded so upset; he wasn't sure who it said it was. "Hello, yes, I can hardly understand you. Stop shouting, calm down and tell me what's the matter. Oh, no. I can't believe it. Don't worry. I'll think of something. Hold on and let me think. Stay where you are. Let me make a call, then I'll come to you. I'll take care of everything. Don't worry. I'll fix it. Just stay put and try to relax. For heaven sake, get cleaned up. I'll be there as soon as I can. Don't answer the door until I tell you it's me at the door."

Mack Stacy, a good friend of Joan's brother, Larry, lived with Joan and Albert for a while. He came home from high school at about 2:45 P.M. and discovered Joan lying in the bathroom. He felt for her pulse and finding none, called the Martinsburg police. Soon police cars raced up the street: "Mack, you did the right thing calling the police first." Police Chief Rob Penhelm told him. "I called Albert, his father, the constable and the first selectman. They should all be here soon," added the Chief. "You didn't touch the gun, did you?" asked the Chief.

"No, I knew not to do that," answered Mack. "I just felt for her pulse." Mack broke down and began to sob. "I didn't touch anything else, just Joan."

"Good thinking. Mack, it's okay, son, you did well. I don't imagine you've ever seen a crime scene before, have you?" said the Chief. Mack shook his head indicating, 'no'.

"Well, let's get to work. Let's check out this scene," suggested the Chief.

Later the Chief, the first selectman, Toby Muzik; the medical examiner, Dr. Griswold and the constable, Walt Nomack were all together at the scene. "Here comes Barbara, Albert's sister," noted Walt Nomack. "I wonder where Albert is," he added.

"I came as soon as I saw all the police cars coming up the street," she said.

That's odd, thought Walt. Since the trees between Albert's house and hers, next door, would have obstructed her view, Barbara couldn't have seen the cars.

The Chief and Barbara soaked up the blood from the floor. He went out to the back porch with the sopping wet, bloody rags and found a pair of bloody sneakers in the trash basket;

Someone had not even attempted to cover them up. However, the investigation was cursory at best as evidence was removed when the blood was cleaned up, some evidence was moved and some was not even collected and preserved. "So many of us handled the gun, we won't be able to get any prints," Walt Nomack told the Chief. "The footprints are messed up too," he added. Walt thought it was very strange that a team that was usually so capable, had done such a poor job of processing the scene of an obvious murder.

The Chief took a call from Albert's father, D. Albert Barron. "Yes, yes, I understand. Don't worry about a thing. Everything is being taken care of. There won't be any problems. We're just about ready to remove the body now. We should be leaving soon. I'll explain it to Toby. I'm sure he'll understand. You've got it. That's mighty generous of you, Mr. Barron." Penhelm ended the call. "Toby, you could probably tell from the call that I got instructions from D. Albert. We're to let her body go to the funeral home, take care of things here and most importantly, keep it all on the QT. If you and I hush everything up, there'll be 2Gs in it, one for each of us. Not bad, huh, for keeping it quiet, for burying the story. No pun intended, Toby," added Penhelm, chuckling.

"No problem at all, Chief," responded Toby Muzik. "When the funeral's over, it's all over. Nothing to it," said Muzik. "Just how did D. Albert get so much control in this town anyway?" he asked.

Chief Penhelm related how Albert's father exerted this much influence due to his standing within the community. "This farmer has land, wealth and influence. He owns a lot of property from apartment houses to Barron Park down by he lake. He has spent his life acquiring more of each, which has provided him with respect and control. D. Albert got what he wanted from those in other positions. People know he means business and they'd better keep quiet for their own good. No one takes a chance by challenging him. He controls his family members too. He bought houses next door to each other for Albert and Barbara. She and Albert have to follow their father's rules to keep them," the Chief explained.

"Walt, you said the gun was here on the kitchen table," said Toby Muzik. It would have been handy for her to use to commit suicide," he added.

Walt Nomack responded, "Yes, Albert told me he put the gun, loaded, on the table but Joan couldn't have committed suicide, put bloody sneakers on the porch and come back in here. Look at this Colt 38. She couldn't have held the gun, turned her wrist and fired at herself. It's impossible. She would've needed to use her thumb to fire it. Besides that, there are no powder burns on her. When women commit suicide, they usually use the exhaust pipe in the car or a stash of pills. Most don't do something to their head or face, especially a good looking woman like her," he added.

The coroner, Dr. Jameswell, asked to speak to Walt Nomack alone. Walt could tell from the look on the Chief's face that he didn't like the idea. He probably wanted he coroner to speak to him, he thought. Dr.

14

Jameswell asked Nomack, "Do you think she committed suicide?"

"Not a chance," answered Nomack. "As I told the others here, there's no way she could have turned that gun around and fired at herself. She would have to use her thumb to fire it. If she had fired two shots, she'd be unconscious from the effort. She would never have fired a third shot. Don't forget there are no powder burns on her," he added.

"I'm glad to hear it. I agree," said Dr. Jameswell. "Looking at the angles of the shots, particularly the one that hit her, there's no way that that her death was a suicide," he added. The Chief of Police insisted that Dr. Jameswell sign the coroner's report indicating that Joan's death was a 'suicide", which he refused to do. In the end, Dr. Jameswell's signature was not on the report and he resigned from his position as coroner over the matter.

Just as Joan's body was about to be removed from her home. Albert arrived and sat in the living room. Walt Nomack asked, "Where is Albert? They are almost ready to take Joan's body out. Doesn't he want to see her? He hasn't so far." He went to ask Albert.

"No, not now, Walt. I'll see her later. You know, after they, after they, take care of her," said Albert. But he never saw her at home, at the funeral home or even just before the funeral.

Walt wondered if Albert thought so little of her that

he didn't want to see her one last time. It looked that way, he thought. He overheard Albert tell the Chief during his interview with him, "If I tell you who did it, I'll be incriminating someone in my family."

———◄○►———

At Joan's wake, mourners said, "She looks so good, you'd never know she'd been shot." Her brother, Larry, tried to console his parents who were beside themselves, crying profusely.

Joan's father said to his buddy, Ben, "If only I hadn't signed permission for her to marry him. She was too young. If only I hadn't given her to Larry and Fiona to raise, she wouldn't have moved to Martinsburg and met Albert." "She told us they were having problems. She didn't see Albert much. He was always out at night. If he wasn't at his sister, Barbara's next door, he was out with the guys," added Larry.

"We tried to help. We babysat to give Joan a break," said Fiona. "We hoped she and Albert would go out and spend some time together," she added.

"We should've known something was wrong when she told us she only had pocket change in her purse," recalled Larry. "Can you believe that's all Albert allowed her to keep?" he asked.

"Where is Albert?" asked Chief Penhelm addressing Walt Nomack. "Oh, I'm sure he'll be along anytime now," answered the constable. He knew Albert as a part-time officer on the police force. "The boy's probably being consoled somewhere out in the lobby. This place is packed."

Mrs. Coulton noticed his absence too." Surely he's coming, that's his wife in there. Where can he be?" she asked.

"Actually, he's at a party at their house with his band tonight," related the minister, Pastor Momert. "He assured me he'd be here for the service tomorrow," he added.

"Albert's having a party!" said Joan's best friend, Belle Brightman. "I can't believe it!" How could he? She thought.

Another of Joan's friends, June McShane, shared Belle's disgust. "How could he indeed with Joan lying in there, gone forever," she mourned.

Albert was at Joan's funeral the next day along with the numerous mourners from the wake the previous night. His sister, Barbara, left immediately after Joan's death for a trip to Florida and was not at the funeral. Their mother, Sophia, held one grandson while D. Albert held the other. Albert showed no emotion and shed no tears. Joan was buried in the Barron family plot, in the grave labeled 'wife'. Plots awaiting D. Albert and Sophia were marked to her right.

During the next few weeks, Chief Penhelm interviewed many people including Joan's parents and her friend, Betsy Mooney, to make it appear as if her death was being investigated. Only a few knew that it was not and never would be fully investigated.

After Joan's death, there were just too many other deaths. It was eerie. Within days of Joan's death, Anna Coulton told her husband, Bill, and Walt Nomack, "I know who killed Joan. Tomorrow I'm going to tell you."

The next day, Walt's neighbor, Tom, said, "Walt, can you believe it? Anna was found strangled with a scarf?" he said. "Suicide was mentioned as the cause of death in the paper but I for one, can't believe it. She was a happy person, not sad or depressed." added Tom.

"She only told two people she knew who did it, her husband and me. I wonder why she didn't tell us, who killed Joan that night," said Walt. "Maybe the wrong person overheard her tell," Walt added.

After some thought, Walt decided it had to be her husband, Bill who killed her. He was related to the Barron family and probably did not want the name of Joan's killer to get out. Anna Coulton's death went uninvestigated also, easily forgotten by some but not by those who mattered.

Within several months of Joan and Anna Coulton's deaths, there were more eerie deaths. Toby Muzik phoned Chief Penhelm, "Can you believe it? D. Albert died yesterday at the relatively young age of sixty-two!" he exclaimed. Three months later, Toby called again; "Chief, you won't believe it. Young Albert Barron's grandmother, Mabel London, moved to Glenville and last night she committed suicide. That family has lost two more members in a few months! What do you make of it?" he asked the Chief.

"Well, it makes me think that they must've been very upset and stressed about someone or something important to them," he answered Toby Muzik.

As time went by many theories developed as to the cause of Joan's death. One theory, which the Barron family continues to believe, is that Joan committed suicide. Albert's sister, Frances, notes that Joan had a slight mental problem, implying Post Partum Depression, similar to her mother's problem after childbirth.

Some residents of Martinsburg believed that Albert murdered Joan. "He'd been seen around town dating more than one woman," said Alma White. "I saw him with Myrna Martin who became his second wife. Some say he dated her before and after he married Joan. I wonder if........Alma's voice trailed off.

"What? What do you wonder? asked her husband, Ed White.

"I wonder if they were in cahoots. I wonder if they plotted to get rid of Joan together," answered Alma.

"Albert wanted out of his marriage and the responsibilities of having two children," Lydia Buckley added.

"I think he wanted to be with his "second wife," said Tom Buckley. "He openly called his sister, Barbara, by that name. Some of his actions just made him look bad. He didn't show any emotion at his wife's funeral; he was expressionless," he said.

"He had a party during her wake and I heard he disposed of all pictures of Joan. What are their baby boys going to look at someday?" asked Tom Jeeter.

Others thought it was Barbara who was the murderer. Constable Walt Nomack saw Albert and Joan as a happy couple when he and his wife had dinner with them. Albert was attentive and he treated Joan nicely. He was the friend who would "give you the shirt off his back", according to Walt. However, Walt also remembered that Joan was only allowed to keep pocket change for herself and was to shop with her sister-in-law Barbara as chaperone. He knew Barbara hated Joan because Albert had indicated as much once in conversation.

Walt became suspicious of Barbara when she quickly showed up at the scene of Joan's murder saying she came as soon as she saw the police cars. She was unable to see them from her house next door.

She also left suddenly for Florida after the murder. Walt was aware that she and Albert had been in a very close relationship for a number of years. "They were so close he openly called her his second wife," he said. "Albert said what he couldn't get from Joan physically, he could get from Barbara. Their relationship was incestuous," he explained.

"Barbara was jealous of Joan's beauty and popularity and she wanted Albert for herself," added Irene Telford. "Maybe she was just tired of sharing him with Joan," she concluded.

The State of Connecticut's Chief Detective, Stan Rhone, was convinced the murderer was Mack Stacy. He called the Chief, "Listen Penhelm, I want you and Nomack to go out to the high school and pick up Mack Stacy. Bring him to me for questioning.," he told him. The Chief and the constable went to Regional #20 Junior-Senior High School and pulled him out of class for questioning. While Rhone questioned Mack, Walt Nomack listened in to the interrogation through the intercom in Stan's office. Hey, what's this, he thought, as he happened to notice a written report on Stan's desk. It's Mack's confession already typed up and ready for his signature. That - - - he thought. This was one of Stan's classic techniques. It was never signed, as even Stan couldn't make the murder charge stick. Mack's alibi was airtight and he did not admit to a crime he didn't commit.

"I still say it could've been Lucien Coulton, brother of Bill, because he was a scary sort of fellow who appears in town occasionally," thought Al Crombly. "His old worn clothes are torn and full of holes. They look like he's worn them day and night and probably, slept in them. His face is dirty and unshaven. When he speaks, you can see his teeth are brown, maybe stained from chewing tobacco. His eyes stare at you with an eerie glint in them. Women say that he undresses them with his eyes. Maybe he even made a pass at Joan and she resisted. That might've made him very angry," he explained.

"Unless he visited her and she angered him, I don't see how there would be a connection between them. It doesn't make much sense to me," said Buzz Hutchins.

———— ◄o► ————

One might wish that Joan had left a clue of some sort as to the identity of her murderer but Joan didn't leave any clues at the scene because she couldn't. She had no time to think of a way and, no way to do so. She never knew how much danger she was in until the moment she saw the figure with the pistol. She knew her marriage was rocky but she never thought she'd be killed. Did she even connect her marriage to this event? Who is to say she ever thought about any connection. The terror she experienced during those few minutes before the last bullet took her life overshadowed any rational thoughts she might have had. A depraved and senseless killing snuffed out her youth.

Was it a suicide or a murder? Suicide was ruled out as a cause of Joan's death by the scant evidence processed at the scene. Was it a murder committed by a single person or was it a conspiracy between two whom wanted Joan out of the way? When all possibilities were considered, there were six scenarios. Single murderers could have included Albert, Barbara, Myrna or Lucien. Albert and Barbara or Albert and Myrna could have conspired.

Larry and Fiona Andrews sat at their kitchen table, sipping their morning coffee. "Remember when Joan first came to us?" asked Larry. "She was the sweetest baby girl even at a few years of age," Larry recalled.

"Of all the girls and boys we've taken in over the years, she and Larry were the best, the nicest and kindest of all," reminisced Fiona. "That's why we adopted them and just fostered the others," said Larry. "There was something special about them right from the start," he added.

"Joan fit right in wherever she went whether it was Brownies, 4-H, Scouts or choir. She played the piano and organ in church so beautifully," added Fiona. "We were so proud when she was inducted into the honor society. She was such a good student. She had a bright future at work and then as a mother."

"Joan was becoming a wonderful mother." We should have encouraged her to leave Albert and taken her in," said Larry.

"We could've made room for her and the boys." Fiona went on. ""We could've helped her make it on her own and we would've still had her with us," she said. Fiona started to cry.

"You're convinced she was killed, but who was the killer?" asked Larry.

"Yes, I am convinced," responded Fiona. "Of course, she was killed. She would never have committed suicide. I really think it was Albert because of the way he treated her." Fiona said.

"I'm not so sure," said Larry. "It could've been Barbara. We know the cops didn't investigate enough. It was open and shut, clear Mack Stacy and declare it was suicide. There's something strange about her. She took off for Florida so fast, she didn't stay for the funeral. She was always with Albert so, where was she when he needed her the most? On a vacation," he noted. "People in town say she was jealous of Joan. Maybe she was so jealous, she wanted her out of the way," he said. "When we saw Barbara and Albert together, it looked like he was her pet. She was usually close by him and always touching him. Barbara was home that day, planning on taking Joan and the boys shopping. She had a key and could've let herself in anytime." said Larry.

"Barbara didn't seem to have much of a life. She had her job, Joan, Albert, her parents and that was all," Fiona summed it up. "She was a loner. She didn't seem to have any friends over to her house."

D. Albert and Sophia Barron sat sipping their coffee after dinner in their formal dining room as they reminisced about raising their four children. "Amelia, Frances and Barbara are each so different, such individuals," remarked Sophia.

"Maybe it's because there's such a difference in age between the three girls and Albert, that he stands out," said D. Albert. "He sure was a surprise after having the three girls years before him. Maybe we raised him differently because he grew up as an only child or because he was a boy," wondered D. Albert.

"You treated him like a king and would have protected him from anything" Sophia added. "He's always had everything he wanted. He thought he wanted to be married. He was too young and he wasn't ready. He doesn't take any responsibility for his sons at all. He assumes I'll do everything," said Sophia. That must be what he did with Joan, she thought. "Albert wants to drive the truck or work the farm and after that, he's out having a good time," Sophia's voice trailed off.

"Maybe I was wrong to sign permission for him to marry," said D. Albert. "He was just too young," he concluded.

"Now we have two more children to raise. Albert's not going to do it," said Sophia. "As much as I love the babies, I'm too old to be their mother," she added. "I'll be eighty-five when Kenny is twenty-one," she said. (Sophia died when Kenny was twenty.)

"We'll have to help each other," said D. Albert. "And get Albert to take on some responsibility for the boys."

"That will be easier said than done," said Sophia.

———◄○►———

To envision how Joan and Albert came to such a devastating end of their relationship, one has to return to the beginning of Joan and Albert's connection. Albert bullied Joan into going out with him by telling her that he would tell their classmates that they had sex. In spite of this, Joan found she liked him and later, loved Albert. Joan and Albert dated steadily through her three years at Region #20 Junior-Senior High school in Herndon, CT. Three towns, Herndon, Adams and Martinsburg, regionalized and opened the new school in September, 1957. In addition to being an honor student and inducted into the W.T. Heimler Chapter of the National Honor Society, Joan worked on her yearbook, the1960 Triad, in the Library Club and as a cheerleader for the soccer and basketball teams. She was beautiful, popular and called "Blondy" due to her medium-length, wavy, natural blonde hair.

Albert was not as active but was in chorus and choir, band and Student Council, each for one year. His yearbook, the1959 Triad, had this quote beneath his picture, "I agree with no man's opinions; I have some of my own." His nickname was the "Shadow".

Albert and Joan waited impatiently for her to graduate so they could marry with their parent's permission at ages eighteen and nineteen. They wanted to be together and no one more so than Albert who told Joan she had better give him what he wanted or he'd tell the whole school that she had "gone all the way with him". No nice girl in 1960 wanted that lie spread among her friends and classmates.

Many senior girls planned to go to nursing school, business school, or college to become teachers. They went to Windall Technical High School to become hairdressers or food service workers. Some received training to become airline stewardesses (they were not yet called flight attendants). Joan's plan was to work as a secretary, which she did at Hartford Hospital, marry in the summer of 1960 and to have her children.

Many senior boys planned to enlist in the armed forces. Some planned to go to college, Windhall Technical High School or other specialized technical school such as the Ward School of Electronics or Porter and Chester Institute. Some went directly to work; some in a family business. Albert's plan was to farm with his father, drive a truck or work construction and to marry Joan in the summer of 1960.

They set their wedding date for August 20,1960 and were married at the Martinsburg Congregational Church, which they attended all of their lives. It was a hot day without a storm cloud in the sky. Joan wore the beautiful gown of her dreams. It was a floor length lace gown designed with a scalloped neckline and full skirt of peau de soie. It ended in a chapel length train. Her elbow length veil was held in place by a crown of iridescent crystals and seed pearls. She carried a bouquet of white roses and stephanotis. Joan's attendants included her best friends. Meg Froman served as her maid of Honor. Her bridesmaids, Betsy Mooney, Belle Brightman, and June Randall were her attendants. Albert's Best Man was Bo Brigham. His friends, Joe Darin, Bill Rydell and Tim Glendon were ushers. She and Albert honeymooned in the Pocono Mountains in a bridal suite with a heart shaped tub and complimentary champagne.

Albert's father bought them a cute little house in Martinsburg. They unpacked wedding gifts and settled down to married life. They were only married five months when they found out Joan was expecting their first child. She was so excited. Albert was less than excited. "You're kidding! Oh, no, it's so soon. Blondy, You won't be any fun anymore" Albert moaned.

"I'll still be fun. The baby isn't coming for seven months," Joan told him. "We can still, you know – , we can still do it for a long time," Joan added. She was so excited. A baby was coming. Her baby was coming. She hadn't thought that she'd be expecting so soon either but somehow Joan knew everything would be just fine.

After a long labor, Joan delivered her first son, Kenneth (named after her father) on October 23, 1961. Just a few weeks later, at Christmas, she was pregnant again. Of course, she didn't know it that soon but by the end of January, there was no question of her pregnancy. She and Albert couldn't believe it happened so soon after Kenny's birth. Their children would be eleven months apart. They had used the rhythm method of birth control based on the calendar and Joan's menstrual period. It had obviously failed them.

September 1962 brought the birth of their second son, Daniel, on the fifteenth. Kenny was eleven months old and was on the move, on his knees. He got into everything. Joan was busy with diapers and bottles, two babies on two schedules. Did the babies nap at the same time to give her some respite? There wasn't a chance. She asked Albert to help her but he only occasionally and grudgingly helped with household chores. (Who was she trying to kid? Imagine Albert cooking, cleaning up, and washing babies or clothes? There was no way.) He seemed to think all of it was "women's work".

Albert had his "rules" Joan had to live by. One day Albert sat her down and explained, "From now on when you go grocery shopping, my sister, Barbara, will go with you. She knows how to shop and she can make sure you get what we need. She will handle the money and pay for the groceries."

"Albert, I can go alone. I'm doing fine with the shopping and I like getting out for a while," Joan said.

"No, Joan, Barbara will go with you. That's the way it is," said Albert.

And that's the way it was. It was Albert's way. Joan had no money except some pocket change. She might have seen that coming when in high school he blackmailed her saying, "If you don't make out with me, I'll tell the whole school that you went even further." No nice girl in 1960 wanted that to happen. He got his own way by bullying her.

Albert thought Joan was ignoring him when he wanted her attention. He said, "It's always the babies, the babies. Kenny needs feeding. Danny needs changing. Danny is crying and needs rocking at night. I need your attention too. I thought we'd have fun the way we did with our friends before the babies were born," he complained.

"It's different now. I love being home with my babies but I would like some time to myself too. You don't seem to understand that. You want to go out and have fun and you do." Joan explained. She noticed how he began to change after he'd been out with his friends. He didn't pay as much attention to the children or her at all. "We rarely spend any time together anymore. It feels as if you're slipping away from me," she told him.

"If you're ready for fun, I'm ready to go," Albert said.

"I need you and I want you but my first priorities

have to be our babies. Can't we compromise and find some way to spend some time together with friends?" Joan asked Albert.

Albert looked at her and didn't reply right away. "Yeah, sure we'll try that, Blondy" he replied. Joan wasn't convinced by his tone that he'd try. She felt like he'd rather go out with his friends than work out time together with her. Two, three years ago, they were in love and she couldn't wait to be married and have his children. How did our relationship change so fast? Joan thought.

Their parents visited and baby-sat for the boys sometimes. Joan went out with Barbara for groceries or to do other errands. She took the babies to the pediatrician. She no longer had any adult interests and she was becoming housebound. This was not the life she dreamed of either. She thought they would be so happy in their little house with their family. She thought that someday she would return to work part-time, maybe when the boys started school. Some mothers worked part-time these days. How would she get back to her dreams? How would she get Albert back home to be with his family? She thought she needed to show him he could be part of the family doing things men do in their home. He had to settle down. He had responsibilities.

They argued. Joan asked, "Couldn't you go out one night each week? How are you going to be a father if you are hardly ever with your sons?"

Albert countered with, "They don't need me now at their ages. There's nothing they can do with me. They can't play ball or ride a bike yet."

"Albert, you don't understand that you can do things for them. If you took them for a few hours sometimes, it would really help me. I could have some time to myself. You could even play with them in the house like I do. You just need to learn how," Joan said.

"I don't know how to play with babies," Albert said. "When they're older, at ten or twelve, I can play with them. I don't play with baby toys," he insisted.

"By that time, I'll be worn out." Joan countered. "I need you, they need you now, not just when they're older," she insisted.

Fall turned into winter, a very long winter in the Barron's home. Albert and Joan had settled into a pattern. She was the mother and the homemaker and Albert was the provider and absentee father, out having fun with the guys.

Albert spent a lot of time next door at Barbara's house. Anytime they had an argument, he was quick to run over there. He seemed to prefer her company to the boys' and Joan's. He told Joan long ago that he and Barbara had been close since she was a teenager and he was about eight years old. Actually, he started spending more time with Barbara when Joan was pregnant with each baby. At the time, she thought he was tired of seeing her so heavy and uncomfortable. She felt unattractive and his leaving the house reinforced that feeling. Every time he left, it seemed as if he left her for Barbara. When they were together more often than he and Joan were, it was kind of creepy, Joan thought. Who was Albert's wife? Was it Joan or Barbara?

When Albert went straight next door to his sister Barbara's house, he often warmed he up to his advances by encouraging her, "Barbara, come on, give your brother some lovin'. I can't take much more of Joan and the crying babies," he pleaded. "I need you." Barbara needed to be coaxed into things so, they sat down on the couch and had drinks while she consoled Albert, listening to him talk about Joan and his life with her. Although Albert wasn't happy with his life, Barbara was jealous of Joan and longed for it. She would gladly live the life Joan had with him. She could help Albert in more ways than one. "You always know how to make a man feel better. You're always ready to go," Albert complimented her before he insisted on what he wanted. After finishing their drinks and re-fills, Albert and Barbara headed toward the bedroom, each with different plans of how to please the other.

Much later, Barbara took her turn at discussing what she wanted but it wasn't about her sexual desires. "Albert, I can't go on like this much longer. I'm tired of sharing you with Joan. You say you're married to her but you're here when you're not out with your friends," she pointed out. "I want us to be together – all the time. Can't you divorce Joan and we'll find a state where we can be married? There must be one of those southern states where you can marry without a lot of questions. We can say we just happen to have the same last name but we're not related. We shouldn't have our own children but we could take yours if you want," Barbara rattled on and on.

"Whoa, Barbara! You have it all planned out don't you? Joan had everything planned too. She would graduate, we'd get married and we'd start a family. I just didn't think all that would happen so fast. I thought it would take years. First of all, Joan won't give me a divorce, I already asked. Second, why would we have to get married? I want my freedom from all this responsibility I have with Joan and two kids. I just want out," said Albert vehemently. "Now let's forget all that for now and get back over here. Come on," he coaxed. "I think we can come up with a plan later that will make both of us happier." Albert convinced her that they could have their good times now and figure it all out later

During one particular argument, Albert said, "Joan, we argue all the time, we don't have much of a marriage any more. We might as well get a divorce," suggested Albert.

"No, I won't hear of it, Albert. It's absolutely un-thinkable to me," Joan said. "Marriage isn't about having a good time. It's work. We have two children to consider. We need to work at making it better," she paused. "How did we come to this? Surely there's a way for us to get together again. Let's talk to the minister, who married us," she suggested. "I love you, Albert and the boys and I need you."

"No!" Albert flatly refused. "I don't see what the minister can do for us. If we work things out, it has to be between the two of us. I don't want him knowing our problems" I'm sure you don't, Joan thought. Albert left the house, slamming the outer door behind him.

Mack Stacy heard some of their arguments and he heard this one too. He came into the room just as Joan was wiping tears from her eyes. "Albert doesn't appreciate you, Joan. He doesn't know how lucky he is to have you," he added. "He used to Mack. he used to tell me how much he loved me, how he couldn't wait until we married so we could be together," Joan told him. "Now he's never here and we're hardly ever together," she added

"He doesn't know what he's missing," noted Mack, moving closer to her. He was making her feel uncomfortable.

"Mack, can I get you a snack? Dinner was a long time ago," said Joan.

"No," he answered. "I'd rather just be with you," he added.

"Mack, don't say things like that. We're friends but

that's all. I'm a lot older than you and I'm married. Why don't you tell me about that girl you were dating, Tina. Have you seen her lately?" Joan asked. I've got to get him talking about something or someone else, she figured. He can't be interested in me. That's all I need to complicate my life, Joan thought.

Mack took the hint although he was not happy about it. He would've appreciated Joan. She was beautiful. When she listened to you, she made you feel you were important and that she tuned out anyone else. How could Albert leave her alone night after night? He would be there for her; he wouldn't leave her. Mack left Joan alone with her thoughts to go and shoot hoops with her brother. Maybe he'd be able to work off his feelings with some exercise.

Joan's friend Betsy Mooney ran into Meg Froman at the strip mall. "Betsy!" said Meg. "It's spreading all over town that Albert Barron is out at night with other girls. Is it true? Or is it a rumor? Joan doesn't know, does she?"

"I sure hope not," said Betsy. "That would be devastating for her. If I see him, I'll give him a piece of my mind. What do you think it means? Is it the end of their marriage? she asked Meg.

"I think they need help," said Meg "They're not together much. Joan's told me she's not as happy as she thought she would be. Joan said she doesn't get out often except with Albert's sister, Barbara. We don't get together very often. We're at work and Joan's at home. Mostly we talk on the phone. Joan doesn't do a lot except take care of the boys. We've got to try to see her more often," added Meg.

People thought Joan didn't know about Albert and the other girls but she heard whispers behind her back and saw people stare at her when she and Barbara shopped. Joan knew something was up but she wasn't exactly sure what it was. She knew it made her feel very uncomfortable.

There was one event that made Joan more aware of being careful, reminded her to lock the screen door when it was open. One day, at nearly sunset, Joan heard a knock on the door. There stood Lucien Coulton, a local, eerie character who roamed around Martinsburg. His old, worn clothes were torn and full of holes. They looked as if they'd been worn many days and nights and probably, slept in as well. His face was unwashed and unshaven, streaked with sweat on this warm day. When he spoke, Joan noticed his teeth were brown, perhaps stained by chewing tobacco. His eyes looked old beyond his years and had an eerie glint as he stared at Joan. He's undressing me with his eyes, she thought.

"Ya got a glass o' water," he asked. "C'mon, purty lady, I's thirsty. It's warm taday," he begged.

Against her better judgment, Joan poured a glass of water and unlocked the door, quickly handing it to him and locking the door again. Coulton almost pushed his way in but she was faster. He didn't like it.

"Ain't ya gonna 'vite me in" Ya all alone?" he asked.

"My husband will be home in about five minutes," Joan replied. "He had to go out but he'll be right back," she assured him. He turned to go and she was relieved when he left. Maybe he was harmless but at that moment, Joan didn't feel safe. Albert and Barbara could always get in to help me as each one has a set of keys to the doors, she thought.

———◄○►———

Albert's father had come to realize that Albert didn't handle money, especially his money, very responsibly. Once when his father gave him money for a new truck, a friend admired it and Albert up and gave it to him without expecting him to return it. When he was out with his friends, if someone needed money, he was the one to not lend, but give it. He'd be the first to buy something a friend needed or wanted with no questions asked. He never expected to have the cost repaid to him. If he wanted something, he'd buy it regardless of bills that were due. In one way, it made Albert seem like a generous friend, a great guy, among his friends. On the other hand, it indicated how irresponsible he could be especially now that he was a husband and father.

Albert's father liked and trusted Joan. He said more than once that she should handle the money, not Albert. He knew that she was dependable and would do a good job paying bills on time. "Albert," he said. "I'm going to put your house in Joan's name. She's very responsible. She had a good job at the hospital that she was doing well at and she's responsible with the children. I think she's the one to own the house," said D. Albert. The younger Albert was not very happy about that!

THE PRESENT

The Barron brothers, Kenny and Danny, didn't see each other often after Kenny moved to Florida. Danny had married, had a family of his own and was kept busy with his life as a firefighter. He didn't have an opportunity to visit Kenny in Florida. They had grown apart because of the distance between them and the directions their lives had taken them.

Danny was the kind and thoughtful one, who as he grew older, wondered about his birth mother. The boys hadn't lived with their father and stepmother. Their paternal grandparents, mostly their grandmother, raised them. Kenny and Danny visited their other grandparents but were closer to those with whom they lived. Their father also visited them yet, it was almost as if they were adopted and saw their birth father occasionally. So Danny wondered, as an adopted child might, about his birth mother, Joan.

He started to ask questions, fortunately, before his grandmother died when he was just twenty years old. "What was my mother, Joan, like? Do you any pictures of her? I've never seen any."

"There was a wedding picture, an album and snapshots but your father wanted all of them destroyed after your mother died," said Sophia Barron. Danny imagined that his father must've been too distraught to keep them, that they would've been reminders of her death not of her life.

His aunt, Frances, asked Veronica Schnelle if she had a way of obtaining some pictures for Joan's sons. Veronica was well known in Martinsburg as the director of Parks and Recreation but she was far more than the director. It seemed she had contacts all over town. She would know where to get pictures. Veronica obtained copies of Joan's high school yearbook pictures for Danny and Kenny.

When Danny and Kenny were preschoolers, they were told their mother died when they were babies. Later, when they were older, their father added that she had hurt herself with a gun. As insight came with age, they came to realize that 'hurt herself with a gun', was a euphemism for suicide. Danny decided to search for some answers to questions that began to gnaw at him like a dog on a bone. After all the years that had passed, Danny was now ready to consider what might have led their mother to commit suicide.

Where should he start? He and his brother were

in their mid-forties. Many of the people alive at the time of his mother's death, including all of his grandparents, were now deceased. Danny spoke by phone to his father, who had been waiting a lifetime, knowing that someday he would have to answer his sons' questions.

"Dad, I've been thinking about my mom, Joan. Some things gnaw at me, Dad. I can't imagine how she could have committed suicide when Kenny and I needed her so much. We were just babies when she died. We can't even remember her. Didn't she want us after she had us? How could she leave us? I'd never leave my children."

His father didn't know how to address his son's questions any more now than he had the last time this subject came up when the boys were much younger. At that time he told them for the first time that Joan shot herself. Like some men, he disliked having to deal with the subject of death. Joan's death was a particularly difficult subject for him to speak about. "As I told both of you before, she was a lot like her own mother. When she had children, she got depressed afterward. It was her hormones or something. That's what happened. She was so depressed that even though she loved you, she must've felt like she needed to leave all of us. She was sick."

Danny just couldn't accept this answer. How could she leave him and his brother if she loved them? He would never leave his wife and children that way. They meant the world to him. He knew that she and his father went to the Martinsburg church as children and were married there. It was where his grandmother took him and his brother too. She told him his mother played the organ there. She must've been a person of faith. How could she commit suicide? Why wouldn't she have gotten some help, he asked himself. He was forgetting that in the 1960's, many people did not reach out to get counseling let alone let anyone know they had done so. Having a mental health issue, admitting the need for help and getting help for it were just a few of the many taboo topics of the day at that time. One kept one's private business to his or herself.

Danny decided to go back to the beginning. Danny wanted to know what happened to Joan. There must be some records of her death. With a search of these records, Danny located permission forms for his parents to marry, signed by each of his grandfathers, their marriage certificate, Joan's death certificate and a copy of the police report. The notations on the last one left a lot to be desired. Little information could be gleaned as descriptions were brief and didn't provide the details Danny thought they would hold. They didn't satisfy his curiosity. He wanted more. There must be more to the story of what happened to Joan.

Danny thought of the friends his mother must've had. His grandmother had told him Joan was pretty, popular, an honor student and a cheerleader. He went back to their high school, Region #20, from which he and his brother, as well as his parents, graduated. He saw her pictures that he still had at home and he read anything he could find about Joan. He looked at his father's yearbook from the previous year for information about him. He couldn't help but notice the difference between his parents. Joan stood out as a doer; someone involved in her schoolwork and extra-curricular activities. She appeared to be so happy. As he had seen before, she was smiling in every picture, even the candid shots. Had having his brother and him changed her so much? His father's book contained his senior photo, a few activities in which he was occasionally involved and nothing more. He didn't seem very involved in school or activities. Danny wondered what he did with his time. Danny and Kenny had been busy in school clubs and sports at school and in town. Their spare time was always filled.

Some people, who lived in town at the time of his mother's death, would still be alive today, thought Danny. He began to question his friends' parents. He found out that the police chief was deceased but the first selectman and the constable at the time were still living. He didn't know where to look for the coroner. Danny couldn't get any other information from his friend's parents. They were cordial but said they didn't know or remember anything else. Danny wondered, 'Didn't they remember anything about his mother's death?' Sometimes, it seemed as if they couldn't wait for him to end his phone call. A few gave excuses such as, "I have something in the oven." or "I have another call that I have to take." or even, "We're expecting company. I've got to go now." After all the years that had passed, they seemed to want to avoid talking about Joan and her death. Perhaps it was human nature not to re-visit the past, he thought.

Next, Danny began searching for his mother and father's friends. That search took longer than the previous paper trail chase took. He scoured his parents' yearbooks again after asking his father by phone, "Dad, who were your friends and mom's friends in high school?"

"What do you want to know that for?" asked his father.

"I want to talk to them about mom," answered Danny. "Maybe they will remember something about her that they can tell me."

"Danny, do you know that old saying, "Let sleeping dogs lie?" asked his father. "They knew us a long time ago. I doubt that they'll remember much. Let's see if I can add anything to what you already know. I told you your mother was pretty, a cheerleader, a good student, she played piano and organ. She worked for a short time as a secretary before you and Kenny were born. She had good friends and a lot of people liked her. What else can I say? End of story, Danny."

Danny felt sure there had to be more to his mother than they knew at this moment. He wanted to know everything about her. There had to be more to her life story. He was sure of it. It was the missing piece and the core of what left him feeling uneasy.

He decided to look for their friends first and Joan's relatives next. Danny's friends told him to look at the cheerleaders and the pictures of the clubs in which Joan was involved in the yearbook. That's where you'll find her friends, they said. Since his father was involved in only a few activities, Danny was not able to find many possible friends in his father's yearbook. He decided to look for those 'boys' and 'girls' who grew up with them in Martinsburg. Maybe he could locate some of them as many remained in the area. Danny found that the girls married long ago and changed their names, sometimes, more than once. The boys were the easiest to locate using the Internet and local telephone books.

Belle Brightman's brother was located easily and Danny asked if he could help him contact Belle. He explained he wanted to know about his mother's life and death, from those who knew her. He thought Belle knew her because they both took business classes. Her brother suggested that Danny should contact her son and leave a message for her. Danny called him and explained again, leaving his phone and e-mail address for Belle. He waited but there was no response. A number of weeks went by and then, Belle e-mailed that Danny could contact her directly. He was ecstatic; his first contact paid off. He e-mailed his list of questions about Joan and waited disap-pointedly when there was no response from Belle.

Danny called Felicia Rand's sister, who happened to be in his own class, and asked for Felicia's phone number. Felicia was a cheerleader; she had to know his mother. While speaking to her, he learned the names of several of his mother's cheerleader friends. He felt as if he hit the jackpot. Felicia reiterated what he heard from his grandmother, Joan was a sweet girl and an honor student. His parents dated all through high school. Felicia and Joan were good friends. He was crestfallen however after he asked her, "What do you think happened to my mother?"

Felicia replied after a long pause, "Joan changed after her marriage and after the birth of you and your brother. She was a very busy, young, mother. I know that she loved each of you. She looked forward to having you. It was a tragedy when she died. I don't think her friends will have much more to say to you. I know her friends think it was a suicide. I'm really sorry to tell you that."

Now Danny thought he understood why Belle didn't quickly respond to his e-mail. She must have been one of his mother's friends. Danny came to learn that they were close friends. She must've been devastated when his mother died. He e-mailed Belle again stating what he now knew and this time, she answered him.

"Why are you digging into the past?" she asked "You must've spoken to your family members about your mother. They must've answered your questions." She finished by saying, "I don't have anything to add about your mother's life or death."

His search continued using the Internet as Danny

located another cheerleader out of state. He wrote to her, unfortunately, without a response. He called Betsy Mooney's brother and explained why he wanted to speak to Betsy. Her brother took his phone number and e-mail and said he'd pass it onto her. Betsy did not respond. He also called Meg Froman's brother and explained the reason for his call to Meg's sister-in-law. She knew there was something Meg never discussed. Danny guessed it might be his mother's death. He knew from Felicia that Meg and his mother were also close friends. Meg's married name was mentioned during their conversation and her hometown phonebook was part of his collection so, Danny wrote Meg a letter. He would let her decide if she would speak to him, but just as before, there was no response.

June McShane was another cheerleader who couldn't be reached. Danny had hoped someone would tell him where she lived so he could call her. Felicia had provided her name but their conversation ended before it revealed a phone number for her.

Felicia must've been correct, Danny concluded. Hs mother's friends did not want to talk to him. Maybe they just didn't know what to say to him. It wasn't that he was a stranger. Of course they would've avoided a stranger. Who would want to speak about a best friend to a stranger? Danny assumed it might be even more difficult speaking to one of Joan's sons. Perhaps his mother's friends didn't want to relive that part of their carefree younger days when their youth was interrupted by a gunshot almost heard around the town. Danny couldn't explain his mother's death in his youth or middle age. It stood to reason then, that his mother's friends recalled the tragedy and could not explain it in their youth or even by the time they reached their golden years.

There were only three men in his father's class that must've grown up with him in Martinsburg. Perhaps the others stayed at East Halldale High School or went to a technical high school when his father switched to Region #20 school as a junior. Danny spoke to two of the three men and each said they hung around with others, not his father. One said he thought Danny's father was fun to work with and was competent at work. He thought that Danny's father knowing how to drive a truck when they were just kids, working in the summer, was really something. He also said Danny's father wasn't into school activities. He didn't know who his friends were in high school. Danny concluded his father's friends were from East Halldale, friends made during his two years at that school.

Danny phoned his father a third time requesting any information he might not have yet shared with him or Kenny. "Danny, I have thought of something. Did I ever tell you or Kenny that your mother had others in her family? She went to live with her aunt and uncle and used their last name. She was born in Bristol and had brothers or sisters in her first family, named Lawson. You know her mother was sick. She and your grandfather couldn't take care of your mother when she was born. That's why she lived in Martinsburg with her aunt and uncle," said his father.

Finally, some new information and from his father! Danny was shocked that his father had divulged something he and Kenny had never heard before. They had family, more family members on their mother's side. His eyes lit up and he couldn't wait to tell Kenny. He could begin a new search, for their roots. They knew about the Barron side of their family but the Andrews or Lawson side of the family could yield a new treasure trove of information.

Danny's search for more information went back to Joan's birth certificate and the city of Bristol. City Hall's records revealed that there were a number of Lawsons in Bristol. The phone book listed their names and addresses. This was too simple to be true. Danny began his phone calls, hoping to find brothers, sisters or other relatives of Joan Lawson. Some were unavailable so, he left messages, which were not returned, again. Some were available but uninterested in speaking to him. Asking politely if each was related to Joan Lawson, they replied directly or through spouses, "No!" Too much time had passed. The people he spoke to did not seem interested in genealogy and family trees. If only Joan's birth parents were still alive, thought Danny. Perhaps she had sisters or brothers but he realized he would probably never know.

A search of the census records for the 1940's was next but what if Joan's four brothers and/or sisters had been split up and lived elsewhere? The records indicated male and female Lawsons but none matched the street address that indicated where his grandfather had lived. Perhaps they moved around as the size of Joan's family increased, decided Danny. If only he had begun his search earlier, if he had information sooner, he might have had more success, concluded Danny.

Continuing to widen his circle of sources, Danny's next informant came by way of a friend whose aunt was married to the constable, Walt Nomack. Danny had heard of Walt and was impressed by his long-term memory when he spoke to him. In fact, the longer they spoke, the easier it seemed to jog Walt's memory of events forty-four years earlier. Walt was nearly eighty years old now and spoke with a husky voice as he searched his memory for facts and names of people in Martinsburg when Joan was alive. Danny was eager to speak to Walt after learning he'd been at the scene of his mother's death.

Danny had made a list of questions. "Walt, tell me about the scene of my mother's death. What did you notice? Who else was there? What can you tell me about the investigation. Why did they think it was suicide?"

Walt answered Danny's questions and related the facts revealed during the brief investigation. He described his direct observations, withholding any speculation on his part. He told Danny how the scene of his mother's death was processed but left Danny to draw his own conclusions.

Danny repeated what Walt told him. "You said that there were no powder burns on my mother. What does that mean?

"Since powder burns are left on the shooter, not the victim of a shooting, it indicates that your mother was not the one who fired the gun," answered Walt. "The angles of the shots fired were also considered," he added. "The coroner believed that the angle of the shot that hit your mother, in particular, indicated that it was not self-inflicted.

"Then she couldn't have committed suicide," Danny uttered, barely audible as he realized the implication. "You also said bloody sneakers were found outside on the porch. She couldn't have shot herself and put them out there," he added, thinking out loud. "I never knew these facts before. That changes everything!" Danny's smile spread over his face slowly but then, his tears fell rapidly. "How could my father tell us, she committed suicide?" asked Danny rhetorically.

"I don't know, Danny," answered Walt, quietly. He waited for Danny to continue, wondering what his next comments would be.

"If she didn't commit suicide, then how did she die?" asked Danny, realizing the obvious answer as he asked the question.

"I think you can answer that for yourself, said Walt, gently. You know, don't you?" He said.

"All of these years, we thought she left us. We couldn't understand why. This changes everything. You must know more. Tell me. Someone must've killed her. What else do you know?"

Walt did not want to get into some details, although they were few and, he did not want to speculate. He continued on with what he knew to be facts, just the facts of the investigation. "The chief detective, Stan Rhone, had been sure it was Mack Stacy but that he couldn't get him to confess to something he didn't do," said Walt. He explained who Mack Stacy was and how he knew Danny's parents. "We pulled Mack out of school and Rhone questioned him but his alibi of being in school was airtight. I saw the confession Rhone had ready on his desk for Mack to sign when I waited in his office." said Walt. "I know the Chief questioned your mother's parents and a friend of hers," he added. Walt thought he'd said all he could say to Danny without revealing other observations and what he believed happened, things he did not wish to share. Since forty-four years had passed, he thought it best to limit what he shared to facts. What good could come from raising more questions about Joan's death? Danny knew the truth, that his mother did not commit suicide. Walt hoped knowing the truth would suffice but realized Danny might find it difficult to accept and he would probably want to search for additional information.

Danny went home to think. Who could have...why would anyone.....have murdered his mother, he wondered. Everyone said how much she was liked, even loved. They agreed that she was pretty, popular, and a good friend to them. Why would anyone want her dead? It must've been an accident, he decided. But who shot her by accident? Did someone threaten her? Did the gun go off by accident? He decided to speak to Walt Nomack again.

By the time Danny spoke to Walt again, he had already spoken to his brother in Florida. Kenny wasn't as driven as Danny was to find out what happened to their mother. He never conceived of the thought that she had been murdered. He always accepted what their father told them, that she committed suicide, and Kenny continued to believe this was the truth.

When Kenny visited their father the next time, Albert maintained, "Walt Nomack is wrong. It 's sad to say but your mother was sick. It was all in her head. Her depression and suicide were shameful; they were something to keep secret," said his father. We can't change what your mother did. It's in the past. Let it stay there. I have had to accept it. I don't want to discuss it again. Talking about it just brings up old, painful memories that won't do any of us any good," he added. Albert hoped this was the last time they would have this discussion.

Kenny phoned Danny after meeting with their father, "I don't want to hear any more about the possibility of mother's death being anything but a suicide."

"I'm disappointed in you, Kenny. "I thought you would believe the 'evidence' I've uncovered. I think it's pretty impressive. I'll continue my search for more information with or without you, Kenny," said Danny, dejectedly. Danny phoned Walt Nomack the next day to continue his search.

Sam Justis was a large, burly man, a police officer in Martinsburg in the 60's and a good friend of Walt Nomack. Walt asked Sam to meet with Danny. Walt did not want to get into another discussion about Joan's death. He had tried hard to keep their conversations focused on the facts and did not want to discuss his other observations or thoughts about Joan's murder.

Sam had lived in Martinsburg for years by the time Kenny and Danny were born. He knew the town and its people well. He knew Albert from the police force and Joan, through him. He was willing to not only share his observations, but also his impressions. Sam described the young Albert in detail and the young Joan as Danny had heard her described so often before.

"Your father left your care to your mother, Danny," said Sam. He went out to enjoy himself while Joan was home with you day and night. Your mother had her friends but she spent much of her time caring for you. She put you first. Your father worked and wanted to have fun with his friends during his free time. His idea of fun didn't include helping to care for you or helping your mother with anything."

At first, Danny listened to Sam's description in disbelief. The man Sam described couldn't be his father. If he was, what kind of father was he? Did he love his sons? Joan loved her sons so very much. But Albert...he wasn't really ready for them, was he? Danny thought. Sam's information painted Albert as a young father not ready for marriage or fatherhood, but it didn't give him any insight into his mother's death.

When their meeting ended, Danny had a different perception of his father as a young man with two babies to support. It wasn't a kind picture that Sam painted of Albert, but it was accurate. He thought Danny deserved to know the truth. Danny and Kenny owed their upbringing to their mother and grandmother. Sam's revelations gave Danny a different side of his father to consider. He had never viewed his father in this way

Sam was unsure just how far he wanted to go while answering Danny's questions. He would rather let the past lie in the past. It might be best for everyone. Danny wanted to meet with Sam a second time and pursue more questions about what happened to Joan. As they sat down together over cups of coffee, Danny dove in and asked, "What do you think happened to my mother, Sam? I've heard about the scene of her death, the investigation and some evidence.

She didn't commit suicide since the evidence indicated it was not possible."

Sam took a long swig of his coffee and let it slide down his throat as he considered how to answer Danny. "It's so long ago, Danny. I wasn't at the scene that afternoon. I wasn't called in. The evidence, such as it was, is probably long gone. Don't think this is like the crime scene investigation on TV. We can't come across the old evidence and look at it again, hoping to have more clues as to what actually happened."

"I don't think you're really ever going to have a clear-cut answer as to who was the perpetrator. Too much time has gone by. Some who could've answered questions are gone. The records are very brief. My best estimate is that someone came in, picked up the gun, shot your mother for whatever reason and got away with it. Maybe it was an accident or maybe there was an argument. No good is going to come from stewing over what might've happened now," summarized Sam.

Danny considered what Sam said and paused before he replied, "I suppose you're right, Sam," he conceded. "Too many years have passed. We'll never know who did it or why, but we do know how she died. I have to accept that I may never know more details of what happened to my mother but at least I now know she didn't commit suicide. It *is* a major relief to know she didn't kill herself," agreed Danny. "I couldn't understand how she could do that. I just knew it wasn't something she would do. It didn't make any sense. I would still like to know more but I've realized I have to accept what we do know. It's all we can expect to find out," Danny concluded.

Sam breathed an inward sigh of relief. He didn't need to go into the many theories that had circulated around town like flies around a wounded animal on the side of the road. Townspeople had finally almost settled down so many years after the shock of Joan's death. He didn't want to have Danny and Kenny go through the turmoil that had filled the town at that time. At least they now knew the truth that their mother had not committed suicide IF they believed Walt and himself. That was their choice; it was up to them. Which was easier for them to live with, suicide or murder?

EPILOGUE

Lawrence Andrews summarized an announcement in a 1966 newspaper for his wife, Fiona. Well, it's been three years since Joan was murdered and Albert has married 'the love of his life", Myrna, it says. Four years later he read again and noted that Albert and Myrna had a son named Craig. A few more years passed and he read that Albert and Myrna had divorced. He also read that Myrna died of a brain aneurysm at age 62 in 2005. Many years went by and he noticed an announcement of Albert's third marriage to Sherri Martin in Florida. Lawrence and Fiona thought fondly of their oldest grandson, Kenny who is also in Florida and the youngest, Danny who lives nearby in Mooley. He is a volunteer firefighter and owns some of his grandfather's and his father's apartment houses. Danny has the reputation of helping anyone at any time. He seems to be most like his mother, Joan. Mack Stacy became a builder while his friend and Joan's brother, Larry, died at age twenty-five in a car versus truck accident in Herndon. He left his wife, Charlene, and two young children. Larry lies buried near Joan in the Martinsburg Cemetery.

Barbara Barron remained in Florida and married Joseph Gowdly. She died sometime between 1984 and 2006. She often sighed as she enjoyed the sun in North Miami Beach. Thanks goodness for her father, D. Albert, and his devious ways. He had taken care of everything. She had a good life; she couldn't complain.

No one was ever charged with a crime or prosecuted in the death of Joan Andrews Barron. D. Albert Barron paid two individuals involved in the cover-up of her death. Of those two, one is deceased and one is alive. Two of the possible suspects in the case are deceased. The others are alive; two of them visit Martinsburg occasionally.

The story of what happened to Joan may have been buried so deeply that it would not even be called a "cold case". Although there is no statute of limitations on murder in the state of Connecticut, it would take proof of a substantial amount of new evidence to re-open the case. Evidence that was not secured properly and evidence that was stored properly has probably been destroyed by now. Few witnesses would be available for questioning although some are still alive.

Justice was not served in the case involving Joan Andrews Barron since no one was ever punished by our justice system for her death. One can only hope that she rests in relative peace due to those who keep her in their hearts and prayers. May this story serve as a tribute to her for all that she suffered during her short life, so quickly snuffed out at age twenty years, eight months. Rest in peace, Joan. You will remain in our hearts and our memories.

Any royalties accrued from the purchase of this book, after expenses are covered, will be donated to organizations which seek to decrease the occurrence with which women become victims of domestic violence or prevent gun violence. Readers who also wish to contribute may consider making contributions to the following organizations:

Salons Against Domestic Abuse Fund: Cut-It-Out Program (www.cutitout.org)

Family Violence Prevention Fund (FVPF) (www.FamilyViolencePreventionFund)

The Nicole Brown Foundation (www.thenicole-brownfoundation.org)

The Brady Campaign To Prevent Gun Violence (www.bradycampaign.org)

Anyone in need of support should contact the National Domestic Violence Hotline at 1-800-799-SAFE (7233).